Disney's POCAHONTAS

Adapted by
Justine Korman

Illustrated by Don Williams

A GOLDEN BOOK • NEW YORK

Western Publishing Company, Inc., Racine, Wisconsin 53404

Listen to the voice of the wind as it tells the story of Pocahontas, the beautiful daughter of Chief Powhatan. Pocahontas loved the land and the many spirits that lived in the animals, the trees, and the wind.

One day Pocahontas visited Grandmother Willow, a wise
old tree spirit. "My father wants me to marry the warrior
Kocoum," Pocahontas told her. "But he is so serious. And
lately I've been dreaming of a spinning arrow."

Grandmother Willow knew there was great wisdom to be
found in dreams. "It is pointing you down your path," she
told Pocahontas.

"But how do I find my path?" Pocahontas wondered.

"If you listen with your heart, you will understand," Grandmother Willow replied. "The spirits that live in all things will guide you."

So Pocahontas listened to the wind and climbed Grandmother Willow's strong branches. Off in the distance she saw some very strange clouds.

But they weren't clouds. They were the white sails of a
ship bringing men from England in search of gold.

As soon as the boat touched shore, a man named John
Smith climbed a tree to see the wild land. There he met
Pocahontas's raccoon friend Meeko.

"Well, you're an odd-looking fellow!" Smith said.

John Smith had a feeling someone else was also nearby, so he hid and watched. Soon Pocahontas came into view. She was the most beautiful young woman he had ever seen! But when she saw him, Pocahontas ran to her canoe as quick as a deer. Smith ran after her.

"Don't go! Please. I won't hurt you," Smith called.
Pocahontas could not understand the words the strange
man spoke. But Grandmother Willow's words echoed in her
mind. So Pocahontas listened with her heart and understood.
She saw that John Smith's heart was kind.

While Pocahontas and John Smith were becoming friends, Smith's shipmates and Pocahontas's tribe were becoming enemies!

Kokoum and the other Indians watched from the shadows as the Englishmen tore up the beautiful land in search of gold for greedy Governor Ratcliffe. Suddenly the governor's dog spotted the Indians and yelped.

"SAVAGES! IT'S AN AMBUSH!" shrieked Ratcliffe when he saw the strange men in their buckskins. "Arm yourselves!"

Shots rang out and an Indian fell to the ground, wounded.

Quickly Kocoum carried the man to safety and ordered the rest of his men back to the village.

When Chief Powhatan saw the injured man, he was enraged. "These beasts invade our shores, destroy the land . . . and now this!" He had Kocoum send messengers to all the other Indian villages. "We will fight these dangerous strangers together," Powhatan told his people.

But even then Pocahontas was talking to her new friend. As they talked, Meeko grabbed Smith's compass.

"What is that?" Pocahontas asked as Meeko ran off.

"It helps you find your way when you are lost," Smith said. "Meeko can keep it. I'll get another one in London."

"London? Is that your village?" Pocahontas asked.

So Smith told her about cities and houses and roads and how his people would show her people a better way to live.

Pocahontas knew her world was more beautiful than any
city. So she showed it to John Smith and told him
how her people were connected to it.
She even took him to Grandmother Willow's glade.
Smith was stunned. "One look at this place and the men
will forget all about digging for gold!" he exclaimed.
"What is gold?" Pocahontas asked, puzzled.
So Smith showed her a gold coin.
"We have no gold here," she told him.

But when Smith tried
to tell Ratcliffe the
Indians had no gold,
the greedy man
wouldn't listen.
"Lies!" he raged.
"We'll get that gold
from them—
even if we
have to take
it by force!"

The braves were just as eager to fight for their land.
"There must be a path that is better than fighting,"
Pocahontas told her father. "If one of the strangers was
willing to talk, would you listen?"
Powhatan said yes.

That night Pocahontas met John Smith in Grandmother Willow's glade and asked him to talk to her father.

At first Smith refused.

Then Grandmother Willow said, "Sometimes the right path is not the easiest one." The wisdom in her words made Smith finally agree.

Pocahontas was so happy, she kissed him!

Two figures watched as they kissed. One was a settler named Thomas. The other was Kocoum.

Angrily Kocoum charged at Smith.
"Kocoum, no!" Pocahontas cried.
Frightened, Thomas fired his musket at Kocoum.
"Run, Thomas!" Smith shouted.
As Thomas fled, Indian warriors swarmed into the glade
and captured John Smith. They gathered up the fallen body
of Kocoum. Back at the village Chief Powhatan told his
people that Smith would die at sunrise.

After Pocahontas heard her father's words, she went to Grandmother Willow. "I thought my dream led me to John Smith," she cried. "But now he is going to die! I feel so lost!"

Just then Meeko dropped a round metal object into her hands. Through her tears Pocahontas saw John Smith's compass. Its needle moved back and forth. "The spinning arrow from my dream!" she whispered.

Grandmother Willow smiled. "It shows you your path! Let the spirits of the earth guide you."

Pocahontas ran like the wind. At daybreak she found John Smith at the edge of a cliff. She threw herself across him and begged her father to spare Smith's life.

"Look around you!" she cried. "This is where the path of hatred has brought us."

Two armies stood ready to fight. The settlers clutched their muskets. The Indians pulled their bowstrings taut.

"I love him," Pocahontas declared. "This is the path I choose, Father. What will yours be?"

Chief Powhatan dropped his weapon. "If there is to be more killing, it will not start with me."

The settlers lowered their guns.

"Now is our chance! Fire!" Ratcliffe commanded.

But none of the settlers would shoot. So Ratcliffe grabbed a musket and aimed at Chief Powhatan.

"No!" John Smith cried as he leaped between the bullet and its mark.

Smith had to return to England to get treatment for his wound. Ratcliffe was returning, too—in chains.

Pocahontas and Smith parted sadly. "Wherever I am, I'll always be with you," Smith told her as he left.

Pocahontas turned her face to the sky. But she did not cry, for she knew they would always be together in their hearts.